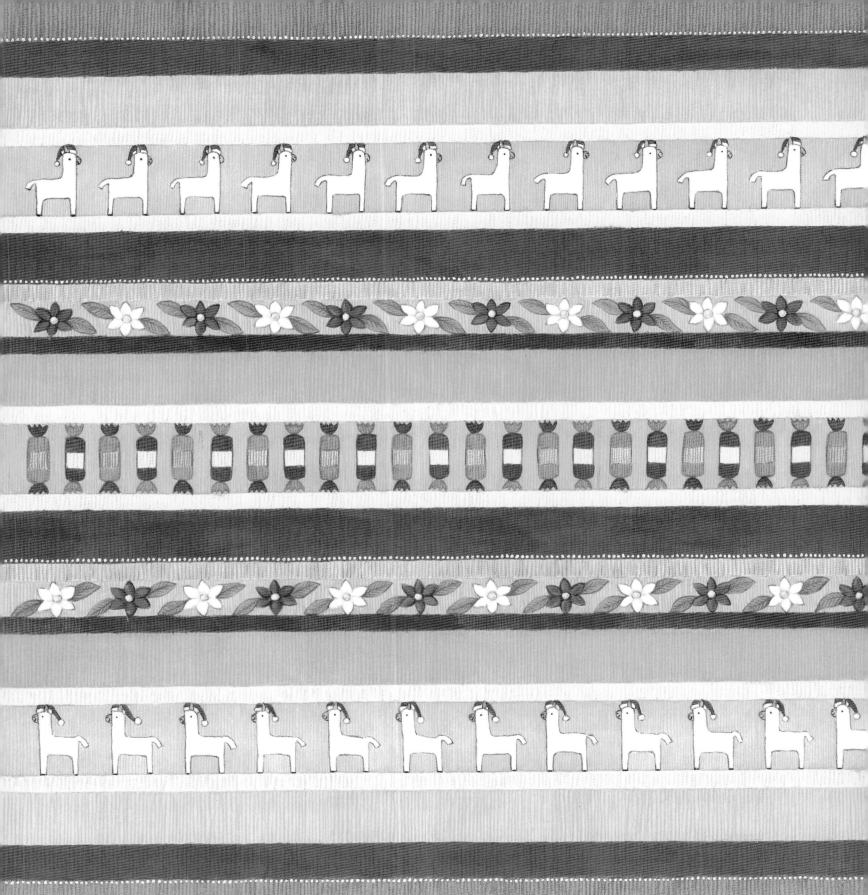

Macca's Christmas Crackers

MATT COSGROVE

For the best presents I ever received,
the Lion and the Hunter — love M.C.

Koala Books
An imprint of Scholastic Australia Pty Limited
PO Box 579 Gosford NSW 2250
ABN 11 000 614 577
www.scholastic.com.au

Part of the Scholastic Group
Sydney · Auckland · New York · Toronto · London · Mexico City
New Delhi · Hong Kong · Buenos Aires · Puerto Rico

Published by Scholastic Australia in 2018
Text copyright © 2018 Matt Cosgrove
Illustrations copyright © 2018 Matt Cosgrove

 A catalogue record for this
book is available from the
NATIONAL LIBRARY OF AUSTRALIA — National Library of Australia

ISBN: 978-1-74299-882-4 (hardback)

Typeset in Mr Dodo featuring Festivo LC.

Printed by Twp Sdn Bhd, Malaysia.

Scholastic Australia's policy, in association with Tien Wah Press,
is to use papers that are renewable and made efficiently from wood grown in
responsibly managed forests, so as to minimise its environmental footprint.

10 9 8 7 6 5 4 3 2   19 20 21 22 / 1

And dress up like . . .

SANTA!

'Coz **Christmas** is here! The **BEST** time of the year!

Macca often confessed
He was Christmas

OBSESSED!

He **jingled** bells
and sang **NOELS!**

He decked the halls,

And floors,

AND walls!

Stockings were strung

and wreaths were hung.

Tinsel was **tangled**
and baubles were **dangled.**

When it came to the tree

Not an inch
was left free.

He scaled new heights with Christmas lights.

'Let it glow...'

But what Macca **loved best**
Of the whole Christmas-fest,
Was his reason for living—
the spirit of giving!

Oh goodness, oh my! There was **so much** to buy!

A **jetski** for Al, his daredevil pal.

Some **dumbbells** for Harmer,

That muscle-mad llama.

For Maxine and Jax, those sax playing yaks,
who loved to be cool—

an inflatable pool!

Alas for our hero,
His savings were . . .

zero!

Macca was **fraught!**
There were gifts
to be bought!

'I need presents
fast!'

(He'd left shopping 'til last.)

Al looked at that frown,
And calmed Macca down.

'You don't need to spend anything on a friend!'

'You're a real angel, Al,'
Macca smiled at his pal.

'Let's **make** what we can!'

So their workshop began.

And those clever alpacas made their own

CHRISTMAS CRACKERS!

After Christmas dinner, everyone was a **winner!**
Beaming proudly, little Macca gave each friend a **cracker.**

'On the count of three, gang,'

And the **crackers** went **1, 2, 3...**

'It's the **best CHRISTMAS** yet!'
Macca sheepishly shrugged,
and then they all ...

...hugged!

(The perfect present didn't cost a single cent!)

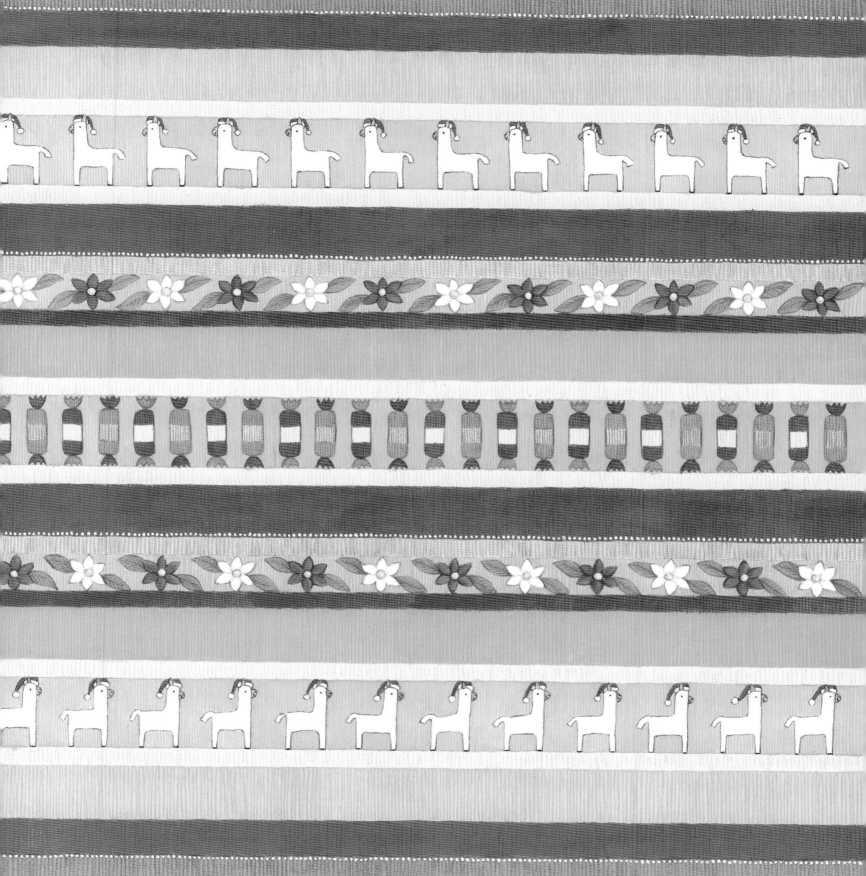

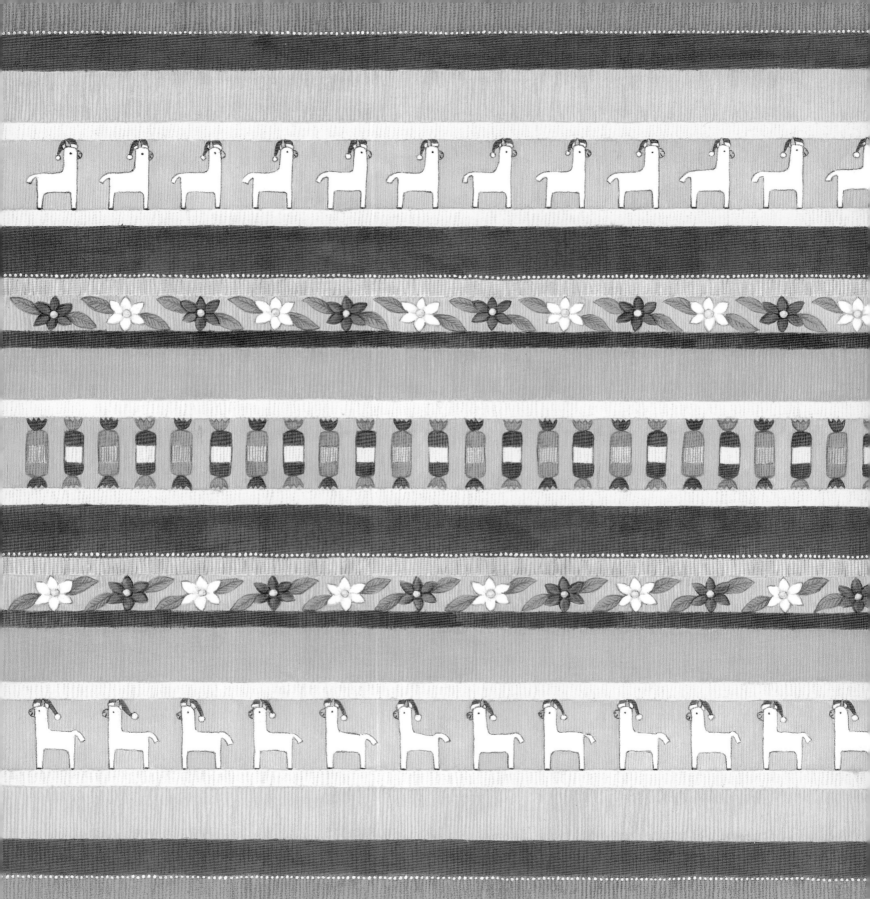